The Zebra

Illustrations: Marcelle Geneste
Text: Nadine Saunier

New York • London • Toronto • Sydney

What do we call the little African horse?

The  – a lively and fast animal.

Its 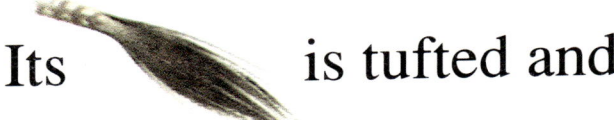 is tufted and

its beautiful coat has

black and white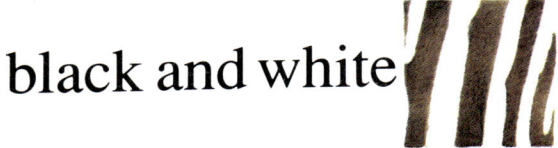

– making it a bright figure on the huge African plains.

Some of the words in this book are replaced by pictures.
These pictures reappear and are identified at the end of the book.

Zebras live in herds
of five to fifteen –
the stallion, his mares, and their young.
They share their feeding grounds

with  and   .

They warn each other of danger –
ostriches have very good eyesight;
buffalos have a very strong sense of smell;

and   have very sharp hearing.

Fights are common among
the herd. In order to
defend their territory,
show their strength,
or attract a mate,
one stallion often challenges another.

Head high, he shows his 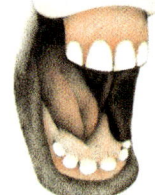 ,

and bites.

The winner rests his head

on the  of the loser.

At mating time,
the  attract the attention of

the males by opening their  .

They seem to be making funny faces!

One year later, an adorable  zebra is born, already weighing about sixty pounds!

The birth takes seven or eight minutes.

The   , unsteady
on its long legs, has to stand up
to be nursed by its mother.
Its coat is thick.

The stripes are
but become darker as the colt grows.
It recognizes its mother by
her smell.

All   are noisy.
They don't whinny like horses;
they bray like donkeys.

They   for hours

and their cry is heard across
the plains, "Ka-ka-ka."
Since they are very hardy,
they are not bothered by the
great heat.

At dawn or at dusk,

zebras look for water.

The lions  them carefully.

The least alert and weakest of the zebras will fall under the lion's   .

Hyenas and wild dogs
are cruel enemies of the zebra.
If the zebras see them,
they flee in terror.

There are  types of zebras,

distinguished by their coats:
The Grevy zebras, which live on the dry, flat land, and are not bothered by thirst or heat; and the
Burchell zebras, which live in

hot   .

In South Africa, the third type,

known as the   zebra, used to be
plentiful. They were able to climb the rocky,

dry
but they have become very rare.
In the wild, these different species
sometimes see each other,
but they never mate.

zebra

tail

stripes

ostriches

buffalos

zebras

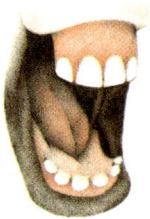
teeth

kick

rear end

females

mouth